P9-DGC-247

Walt Disney's CLASSIC

WALT DISNEY'S CLASSIC

THE RESCUERS DOWN UNDER

Based on Disney's
full-length animated movie

Adapted by A.L. Singer

Featuring characters from the Disney film
suggested by the books by Margery Sharp,
The Rescuers and *Miss Bianca*,
published by Little, Brown & Company.

SCHOLASTIC INC.
New York Toronto London Auckland Sydney

No part of this publication may be reproduced in whole or in part, or stored in a retrieval system, or transmitted in any form or by any means, electronic, mechanical, photocopying, recording, or otherwise, without written permission of the publisher. For information regarding permission, write to Scholastic Inc., 730 Broadway, New York, NY 10003.

ISBN 0-590-44365-8

© 1990 The Walt Disney Company.
All rights reserved. Published by Scholastic Inc.

12 11 10 9 8 7 6 5 4 3 2 1   0 1 2 3 4 5/9

Printed in the U.S.A.   40

First Scholastic printing, November 1990

1

Hrrrrrr!
The low, droning sound rose into the air. It hung over the trees and echoed through the cliffs.

In Australia, otherwise known as the "Land Down Under," the sun was just rising. It peeked over a vast, rocky wilderness called the outback. In the last moments of darkness, everything was silent.

Everything, that is, except the strange noise.

Hrrrrrr!

On the edge of the outback, in a small house, a young boy slept. The sound wafted through his window. *It's only part of my dream*, he thought.

Or was it?

Hrrrrrr!

The sound was louder now. The boy's eyes flew open. He ran to the window and looked into the orange glow of the early morning.

It *wasn't* a dream. He knew exactly what the

1

sound was. It was summoning him, and he knew he had to obey — right away.

In seconds, he was dressed. He slung his backpack over his shoulder, then grabbed a pocketknife. Where he was going, he just might need that.

He tiptoed past the kitchen. His mother was making breakfast, her back toward him. He might make it to the door if he was quiet enough. . . .

No such luck. "Cody?" she asked.

"Yeah, Mom?" Cody replied.

"What about breakfast?"

Cody said, "I've got sandwiches in my pack!"

"Be home for supper."

"No worries, Mom!" Cody ran out the door.

He sped through the outback toward the sound. Along the way, friends joined him — a flock of birds, an echidna named Nelson, and a family of small wombats. Cody loved the animals of the outback, and they loved him, too. Now, when there was an emergency, they were gathering to help him.

Hrrrrrr!

"I know!" Cody yelled. "I'm coming!"

Cody and his friends crashed through bushes. They hopped over logs; they swung from tree limbs.

At the end of their journey was a clearing. And in the center of it, a kangaroo was blowing into a hollow branch of a fallen log.

2

Hrrrrr! came the alarm for the last time. The kangaroo looked up at Cody with relief.

"Who's been caught, Faloo?" Cody asked.

The animals looked at Faloo expectantly. "You don't know her, Cody," the kangaroo replied. "Her name is Marahute, the great golden eagle."

"Where is she?" Cody asked.

"High on a cliff, in a poacher's trap," Faloo said. "You're the only one who can reach her."

"I'll get her loose," Cody vowed.

Faloo smiled. "Right-o! Hop on!"

Cody climbed on Faloo's back. As the kangaroo bounded through the forest, Cody held tight. The animals scurried behind as fast as they could.

Faloo hopped for miles, stopping at the bottom of a steep cliff. Cody looked up . . . and up . . . and up. He gulped. The cliff seemed to rise for miles.

"She's up on top of that ridge," Faloo said.

Without saying a word, Cody climbed off the kangaroo's back.

Faloo looked at Cody with concern. "Be careful, little friend."

"No worries," Cody replied.

But worry was on all the animals' faces as Cody began his climb. Hand over hand, he scaled the rocky wall. A gale wind blew him one way and then the other. He gritted his teeth and dug his fingers in. When he glanced down, his friends looked as small as poppy seeds.

It seemed like hours before he reached the top. He clasped his fingers on the edge of the cliff. Except for the deafening roar of the wind, there was no sound. Could Marahute already be . . . ?

Cody lifted himself up and peered over the side.

For that moment he forgot about the wind. He forgot that he was hanging on for dear life. Nothing else mattered but what he saw.

"Marahute . . ." The word came out of his mouth like a whispered prayer. Cody loved all animals, but he had never seen one as beautiful as this. Her long feathers shone like spun gold, her beak curved regally.

Marahute was meant to stand proud, to soar through the skies. Instead, she was on the ground in a tangle of rope. Her body was limp and lifeless, her eyes barely open. Cody climbed onto the ledge and reached tenderly toward her.

Suddenly Marahute sprang to life. Her body jerked as she struggled to free herself.

"Calm down," Cody said, taking out his pocketknife. "I'm not going to hurt you."

Seeing the knife, Marahute panicked. She shook and twisted, but Cody patiently cut the ropes around her head. He worked his way down, but before he could slice through the final rope, Marahute burst free.

Cody tried to back away to give her room. But he didn't move fast enough. With a thrust of her powerful wings, Marahute pushed him aside. As she flew into the air, Cody lost his balance.

There was no place to go. Cody windmilled his arms, but the ground gave way beneath him.

With a helpless scream, Cody plunged over the edge of the cliff.

2

*F*ooosh! A shadow swooped by Cody's eyes, but he barely noticed. The ground was coming closer. He was going to crash. . . .

With a *thud*, Cody landed.

He opened his eyes. He was alive — *alive!* But something was wrong. Clouds were whipping by him. He felt as if he were floating. And the ground didn't feel like ground. It felt like . . . feathers!

Instantly Cody realized what had happened. He'd been rescued by Marahute!

With a screech, Marahute soared upward, carrying Cody on her back. A grin broke across Cody's face. "WHOOOOOA!" he yelled.

Thwwwockk! Just then Marahute flew into a sharp wind. Cody fell off and began tumbling again.

"Yiiii!" he shouted, his eyes wide with shock. But in a split second he felt Marahute's talons close gently around his arms, lifting him up.

Cody felt relieved — until Marahute began to dive right toward a rushing river! Cody braced himself for the crash. Inches from the river, Marahute let go.

Cody's feet slapped the water. But instead of sinking, he was moving forward. Fast. He felt the wind rushing through his hair, and he gasped with wonder. He was skiing — on his own two feet!

But even *that* thrill didn't last very long. In seconds, he shot out over a waterfall!

Again Marahute swooped underneath Cody and carried him from danger. He held tight as she soared upward along the canyon wall.

At the top was Marahute's nest.

Marahute set him down beside it, at the edge of the cliff. As she walked to the nest, Cody looked over the side. The river looked like a tiny stream between the canyon walls. "Wow!" he murmured.

Just then Marahute's wing swept around him, pulling him toward the nest. His eyes lit up when he saw the eggs inside. "You're a mom!" he said. "Are they going to hatch soon?"

Marahute nodded proudly.

"Where's the daddy eagle?" Cody asked.

When he saw Marahute's sad expression, he reached out to pat her head. He knew just how she felt. "My dad's gone, too," he said gently.

A few huge feathers that had been lining the nest blew past Cody. He grabbed one and began playing with it, but quickly put it back.

Marahute turned her head to the nest and grabbed the feather in her beak.

Slowly she held it out to Cody. It was her gift to him, a way of saying thank you.

Cody took the feather and threw his arms around Marahute's strong neck.

He had made many animal friends before, but this one was special. This friend, in a funny way, was a lot like him.

When Marahute returned Cody to the forest, he was spilling over with happiness. The eagle screeched a good-bye as she flew away.

"*Screech!*" Cody repeated, trying to imitate her. He ran through the forest, gliding like a bird. Marahute's feather, which he had stuck in his backpack, bounced up and down.

In his excitement, he never noticed a sign on a nearby tree that said WANTED: PERCIVAL MCLEACH.

Ting-ling-ling-ling.

Cody stopped. He was used to all kinds of sounds in the forest . . . but not a *bell.*

Ting-ling-ling-ling. Cody spotted the bell right away. It was tied to a small twig sticking out of the ground. A mouse dangled from the twig with a string around his belly. He grunted desperately as he tried to free himself.

Cody kneeled next to the mouse. "What happened to you?" he said, reaching out to untie the string.

The mouse looked startled. "Oh, no!" he exclaimed. "Hey, hey, get away! No!"

"Don't worry," Cody said, "I'll get you loose."

"It's a trap!" the mouse shouted. "It's a — "

But it was too late. As soon as Cody touched the twig, the ground gave way. He and the mouse plunged head over heels into a deep hole!

3

Cody hit bottom with a *thump*. The mouse was able to catch himself at the edge of the hole.

"Are you all right?" the mouse asked.

"Yeah," Cody replied, "I think so." He knew that they had fallen into a poacher's trap — and Cody couldn't stand poachers. They trapped wild animals, then sold the poor animals illegally.

"Be right back," the mouse said, scampering up and out of the hole. Moments later a vine appeared over the top. It dropped downward, inch by inch.

"That's great," Cody shouted up. "Just a little more, a little farther." He reached up and grabbed the tip. But as he climbed up the vine, a rumbling noise made him stop.

"Uh-oh," came the mouse's squeaky voice. Frantically he began to climb back down the vine.

Snnnap! He only got halfway before the vine broke loose. As he tumbled to the ground, a shadowy face appeared over the top of the hole.

"Grrrrr . . ." The face was leathery and fierce, with a long, tapered snout. As it growled, a forked tongue darted out. Cody recognized it right away — a type of lizard called *goanna*, and it was huge!

"Well, Joanna," came a raspy voice. "What did we get today — a dingo, a fat old razorback hog, or a nice big . . ."

A man's face peered over the edge — the same man who was on the WANTED: PERCIVAL MCLEACH sign. He wore a wide-brimmed hat with a feather stuck in it. His chin jutted forward, almost touching his crooked, overhanging nose. The chin and nose seemed to have squashed his mouth into a permanent, ugly snarl. But his eyes were the most chilling part of him — cold, glaring, and evil.

Cody gasped when he saw the long shotgun in McLeach's hands.

"A *boy?*" McLeach said. For a moment he looked confused, even scared. Then he gave the lizard a swift kick. "Joanna, you been digging holes out here again?" he scolded. He turned to Cody and said, "That dumb lizard's always trying to bury squirrels out here!"

Cody could tell McLeach was lying. "No," he said, "it's a trap, and poaching's against the law!"

"Trap? Where'd you get an idea like that, boy?" McLeach replied, shoving his gun down into the hole.

11

Cody felt his heart skip a beat. He put his hands over his face.

"Well, come on," McLeach called down. "Grab a hold. We'll get you out of this old lizard hole."

Breathing a sigh of relief, Cody grabbed the gun barrel. As McLeach pulled him up, neither of them noticed the mouse hopping into Cody's backpack.

Cody climbed over the top. Out of the corner of his eye, he could see what had made the rumbling noise. McLeach had come in an enormous vehicle that was a cross between a tank and a crane. It was as ugly and sinister-looking as McLeach himself.

Cody stood tall and looked up at the man. "This is a poacher's trap, and you're a poacher!"

McLeach knelt down, glaring at him. "True enough, but if I ever find out that you told anyone about this . . . why, I'll come after you and track you down like an animal and skin you alive!"

Just then the mouse stuck his head out of the pack. Joanna pounced on Cody's back. Caught off balance, Cody fell against McLeach.

And McLeach tumbled headfirst into the hole!

"Cut it out!" Cody shouted, fighting off Joanna. "Get off me!"

Inside the hole, McLeach was practically spitting with anger. As he clawed his way out, he muttered through clenched teeth, "I'm gonna kill that dumb, slimy, egg-sucking salamander!"

He scrambled over the top, grabbed his gun, and pointed it at Joanna. He tried to keep a steady aim, but it was impossible. Joanna and Cody were wrestling each other, squirming and rolling. . . .

And that's when McLeach saw the golden eagle feather sticking out of Cody's backpack. His eyes bulged out. He'd already stolen one eagle and sold it for a fortune. If he could get another . . .

Putting his gun down, he grabbed Cody by the backpack and pulled him away from Joanna. "Say, where'd you get this pretty feather, boy?" he asked, yanking the feather out of Cody's pack.

"It was a present," Cody answered.

"Oh, that's real nice," McLeach answered. "Who gave it to you?"

"It's a secret!" Cody retorted.

McLeach reached into his own shirt and pulled out another feather. "That's no secret, boy," he said with an evil grin. "You see, I already got the father!" He pulled the feather across his neck, pretending it was a knife.

Cody's mouth dropped open in shock. So *that's* what happened to Marahute's husband!

McLeach laughed. "Now, you just tell me where Mama and those little eggs are!"

Cody wriggled out of his backpack and fell to the ground. "No!" he yelled, running away as fast as he could.

The mouse jumped out of the pack and scampered off. But McLeach couldn't have cared less about him. He pointed after Cody. "Joanna, sic him!"

Cody's feet barely touched the ground as he ran through the woods. He could hear Joanna's heavy breathing behind him. Through the trees, he thought he saw a clearing. He sped toward it. If it was an open field, he'd be in great shape. . . .

It wasn't.

Cody had to force himself to stop. The clearing ended at the edge of another steep cliff. As he tried to keep from falling over, he looked down.

At the bottom, crocodiles slid into the river. They looked up at him with hungry eyes.

Thrrrassh! Behind him, Joanna crashed through the bushes. Cody jammed his hand into his pocket and pulled out his knife, but it fell to the ground. He dove for it.

His fingers closed around the handle — just as a heavy boot slammed down on his hand.

Cody looked up into the twisted face of McLeach. "You're coming with me, boy," McLeach growled.

"My mom will call the rangers!" Cody said.

McLeach lifted his foot and picked up the knife. "Oh, no!" he said, pretending to be afraid, "not the *rangers!* What'll I do?"

He took Cody's pack and flung it over the cliff. The crocodiles swam greedily into position and waited. When the pack splashed into the water, they tore it to shreds with their razor-sharp teeth.

14

McLeach was practically rocking with laughter. "That's what the rangers are going to find!" He clamped his arm on Cody's shoulder. "Let's go, boy!"

As McLeach pushed him back into the woods, Cody tried to think of a way to escape. But he had lost everything. Even his animal friends were nowhere to be seen.

Slowly his heart sank. There was nothing he could do. Absolutely nothing.

4

The Bushwacker was the meanest-looking vehicle in the outback. Instead of a front bumper, it had a huge metal claw. In front it was a truck, but in back it was a large cage that rolled on treads like a bulldozer. On top of the cage was a long crane.

From a hole beside a tree, the mouse watched McLeach push Cody into the Bushwacker's cage. When McLeach drove away with Joanna next to him, the mouse sprang into action.

He scurried through the woods and dove into another hole. Then he burrowed through a long tunnel and popped into a small room — the official mouse telegraph room of the outback.

"Send for help!" the mouse blurted out. "McLeach took a little boy!"

A mouse telegraph operator spun around and began tapping a message in Morse code. The message took to the air. From mouse relay station to mouse relay station, it raced around the world.

In each place, mice sent the message on. They all knew that no ordinary method could save Cody. This was a case for the bravest group of mice in the known world — the Rescue Aid Society.

CODE RED! ATTENTION ALL R.A.S. DELEGATES! EMERGENCY MEETING IN MAIN ASSEMBLY HALL! The message rang through the basement of the United Nations building in New York City. For humans, that building is a place to discuss the world's problems. For the Rescue Aid Society, or R.A.S., its basement was a place to talk about rescuing humans.

As the mice scampered in, the chairmouse pounded his gavel on the podium. "There has been a kidnapping in Australia," he announced. "A young boy needs our help."

The mice began to murmur, but the chairmouse continued. "This mission will require our very finest, and I know we are all thinking of the same two mice. . . ." He looked around for Bernard and Miss Bianca. Bernard was a rough-and-tumble pantry mouse, who was in love with the elegant Miss Bianca. Together, the two of them had performed feats of bravery no one else would dare to try.

But today, their seats were empty.

"They're gone?" the chairmouse said. "We must find Bernard and Miss Bianca at once!"

* * *

In a restaurant in the same building, Bernard fiddled with his fork. The French bistro had seemed like the perfect spot to propose marriage to Miss Bianca. It was hidden on top of a crystal chandelier in a human restaurant, and it had a romantic view of the city. The food was prepared by insects who took it from the humans below, so it *had* to be good.

Bernard had rehearsed the proposal over and over in his head, and Miss Bianca was smiling and happy. Everything was perfect, but somehow Bernard just couldn't bring himself to say the words.

"You've been very quiet this evening," Miss Bianca said as she finished her main course. "Is there something on your mind?"

Bernard took a deep breath. He reached into his jacket pocket for the engagement ring he had bought. "Well, uh, actually, I . . . uh, I was wondering. . . ."

"Yes, darling?" Miss Bianca asked.

"I, uh . . . Miss Bianca, would you . . ." Uh-oh. There was a *hole* in the pocket! As he touched the ring, he felt it slip through and fall to the floor. "Would you . . . would you excuse me for a minute?"

Bernard chased after the ring as it rolled under another table. A moment later the insect head-waiter ran to Miss Bianca's table. "Pardon me," he said with quiet urgency, "I have important news."

"What is it, François?" Miss Bianca replied.

"You and Bernard have been asked to accept a dangerous mission to Australia." François handed her a note from the chairmouse, which she quickly read.

"Why, the poor boy!" she said, learning about Cody's kidnapping. "I must tell Bernard at once!"

"Allow me, *mademoiselle*!" François answered. "I will tell him immediately."

At a table across the room, an older female mouse sat stuffily with her skinny, shy male companion. When she felt something brush her foot, she slapped her companion for being so forward.

She didn't know what she had *really* felt — Bernard! He had found the ring hanging on her toe under the table, and he had snatched it away.

As Bernard ran back toward Miss Bianca, practicing his proposal, François finally spotted him. "Quickly, Mr. Bernard," François called out. "I must speak with you!"

"Not now, François!" Bernard said. "I'm busy!"

"No, no, no, *monsieur*!" François insisted, running after him. "You don't under — "

With a huge *crash*, François barreled into another waiter, sending trays flying into the air.

Bernard was concentrating too hard to notice. He ran to Miss Bianca and took a deep breath.

But Miss Bianca spoke first. "Bernard, did you talk to François?"

"Uh, yes, but there's something I want to — " Bernard began.

"I know exactly what you're going to say," Miss Bianca interrupted, thinking of the note.

"You do?"

"François told me all about it."

Bernard was flabbergasted. "How did he — ?"

"Oh, it does not matter," Miss Bianca said. "I think it's a marvelous idea!"

"You do?" Bernard said, suddenly overcome with joy. "I mean, you really want to?"

She looked deeply into his eyes. "I don't think it's a matter of *wanting*. It's a matter of duty!"

"D-Duty?" Bernard wasn't sure whether to be pleased or confused. "I — I never thought of it — well, all right. How does next April sound to you?"

"Heavens, no!" Miss Bianca shot back. "We must act immediately — tonight!"

Miss Bianca stood up and walked toward the exit. Bernard followed behind her, saying, "Miss Bianca, this is so sudden. I mean, don't you at least need a gown or something?"

"No, just a pair of hiking boots."

Bernard didn't know *what* to make of that. His head was spinning as the two of them walked through a pipe that led to the R.A.S. headquarters.

"Ah, there you are!" the chairmouse said, leading them onto the podium. "Come along!"

Miss Bianca smiled and took the microphone. Casting a glance over the crowd, she said, "Delegates, we have an important announcement."

Bernard blushed. He hadn't expected Miss Bianca to tell *everyone* about their engagement.

"Bernard and I," Miss Bianca continued, "have decided to accept the mission to Australia!"

"Australia?" Bernard's heart sank. He realized Miss Bianca had misunderstood him.

But worst of all, he realized their lives were about to be turned upside down.

5

Bernard shivered. The rooftop was covered with snowdrifts, and the wind made it hard for Miss Bianca and him to walk.

The wind blew an ALBATROSS AIR sign off a small building. "Miss Bianca," Bernard said, "I'm not sure it's such a good idea to fly this soon after eating." *Especially on a bird's back*, he thought.

"Darling, you'll be fine," Miss Bianca said. "Just knock on the door."

Nervously he gave the door a light tap.

Whuuuuump! An avalanche of snow fell off the building and buried him.

Miss Bianca turned around. "Bernard, this is no time to play in the snow!"

"I wasn't!" Bernard protested. "It was an — "

"Oh, look!" Miss Bianca said, pointing upward.

Where the snow had fallen, a sign now showed: UNDER NEW MANAGEMENT. SEE WILBUR.

Miss Bianca spotted a bird-sized airplane

hangar in the distance. "Let's go there, darling," she said.

Brushing himself off, Bernard followed her. As they got closer, they could hear rock music. They climbed to the top of the hangar door and peered through a hole. Inside was a bizarre sight — a huge bird wearing sunglasses, singing, dancing, and playing air guitar to a loud boom box.

Bernard grimaced. To put it mildly, this bird *wasn't* going to win a dance contest. And if Wilbur was this clumsy on the ground . . .

The two mice slid down an electrical cord into the room. "Hello!" Miss Bianca called out.

But Wilbur just spun around and continued singing.

Bernard raced across the room and turned off the boom box.

Wilbur stopped in the middle of a dance step. "Hey! Who killed the music?"

"Excuse us," Miss Bianca replied. "We're from the Rescue Aid Society. I am Miss Bianca. . . ."

"Miss Bianca? *The* Miss Bianca?" He fell to his knees and kissed her hand. "I don't believe it! My brother Orville told me all about you. This is an honor!" He kissed her hand again. "May I just say — "

Bernard was getting tired of this display. "A-*hem!*" he said, clearing his throat as loud as he could. He walked right up to Wilbur and stared him in the eyes. "We need to charter a flight."

Wilbur's smile broadened. "Well, you've come to the right place, buddy boy! Albatross Air — a fair fare from here to there! I've got tons of destinations. Faraway places, custom-designed for a romantic weekend getaway. . . ."

Bernard cringed as Wilbur dumped an armload of brochures on him and Miss Bianca. ". . . as well as the finest in-flight accommodations. Speaking of which, what can I get you?" He reached into a cooler. "How about a Mango Maui punch? Very nice — "

"Uh, no, thank you," Miss Bianca said.

"Now look," Bernard interrupted. "We need a flight to Australia."

"Australia? The Land Down Under?" Wilbur took a drink and walked over to a wall calendar. "That's a fabulous idea. So when can I pencil you in? After the spring thaw? Mid-June would be nice."

"Oh, no," Miss Bianca said. "We must leave tonight!"

Wilbur immediately choked on his drink. "Tonight?" he sputtered. "Come on, you're kidding me, right? Have you looked outside? It's suicide out there. Oh, no. I'm afraid your jolly little holiday will have to wait." He laughed nervously.

"But you don't understand," Miss Bianca pleaded. "A little boy needs our help. He's in trouble."

Wilbur stopped laughing. He let the words sink

in. "Boy? You mean, *little kid* kind of boy?"

"He was kidnapped," Miss Bianca said.

"Kidnapped?" Wilbur repeated, with a look of shock. "Oh, that's awful, locking up a little kid. Kids should be free. Free to run wild around the house on Saturday morning. Free to have cookies and milk and get those little white mustaches. Nobody's gonna take a kid's freedom away while I'm around — *nobody*, hear me?" Wilbur was revved up. He gestured wildly with his wings.

"So you'll take us?" Miss Bianca asked.

Wilbur snapped into a military salute. "Storm or no storm, Albatross Air at your service!"

In moments, Bernard and Miss Bianca were in their compartment — a sardine can strapped to Wilbur's back. As they fastened their seat belts, Bernard began to feel less afraid.

"Okay, we'll be departing following our standard preflight maintenance," Wilbur said. Suddenly Bernard and Miss Bianca felt as if they were in an earthquake. Wilbur was doing jumping jacks! "Yeah, loosen up! Get the blood flowing!" He touched his toes, then twisted to the left and right. . . .

Crrrrack! Bernard felt a sharp jolt as Wilbur threw his back out.

"Aieeee!" Wilbur shouted. Quickly he straightened out. "Yeah, that feels better. Oh, baby. Okay, sports fans, let's go for it!"

He went to the hangar door and flung it open.

With a deafening roar, the wind rushed into the room. It tossed Wilbur around as he tried to run down the runway. "Whoa, hey, I didn't adjust for the wind," he said. "Whoa! Hey, slippery . . . we got ice! Hang on, uh, here — here we go. . . ."

With a loud "Kowabunga!" Wilbur finally left the ground.

Bernard felt the blood rushing from his face. He was terrified. Beside him, Miss Bianca shivered with happy anticipation. "Captain," she called out, "is this a nonstop flight to Australia?"

"Well, not exactly," Wilbur answered, flapping his wings against the strong wind. "No — uh, no, no, I could definitely say no."

Bernard gulped. His only hope was that their first "stop" wasn't a crash landing!

"Well, we've got to hurry," Miss Bianca insisted. "There's no telling what the poor boy must be going through."

Miss Bianca was right. Half a world away, McLeach's Bushwacker roared across a desolate part of the outback. Cody looked out helplessly through his cage. He had heard about this area. Years ago people used to dig here for opal, a precious stone. Now the opal mines were dark and abandoned. It looked like no one had been here for ages.

"Look around, you stupid pup," McLeach snarled. "Dead ahead is home, sweet home."

Cody's eyes widened. Ahead was a sinister, abandoned mine. It sure didn't look like a home.

Across the outback, Cody's mom looked into the backyard. Her brow was creased with concern. "Cody!" she called out. "Cody?"
There was no answer.

6

"Ladies and gentlemen, welcome to Australia. We are beginning our approach to Sydney Airport. . . ."

Bernard and Miss Bianca awoke when they heard the muffled voice over the loudspeaker. "Perhaps we should wake Wilbur," Miss Bianca said with a smile.

They looked down to see Wilbur asleep on a huge tire. Their trip had been smooth — but only because Wilbur had stowed away on a jet airplane in New York. They had flown to Australia in the compartment where the landing wheels were stored.

"Wilbur!" Bernard called out. "Wilbur?"

Wilbur stood up and stretched. "Okay, I'm up, I'm up."

Just then the floor below them began to move. A trapdoor was opening to let out the landing wheels. Wilbur grinned. He put on his goggles and prepared to dive. "Put another shrimp on the

barbie, girls," he shouted, " 'cause here we come!"

"Here we go again," Bernard muttered.

"Cannonball!" Wilbur cried, diving through the trapdoor.

Bernard and Miss Bianca held on tightly as he flew among the buildings of Australia's largest city, Sydney. "Next stop, Mugwomp Flats!"

Bernard sighed. Mugwomp. It sounded like just the kind of place they'd end up in with Wilbur.

"Mugwomp Tower, this is Albatross One-Three requesting permission to land. Over."

The voice came over the loudspeaker on the roof of a long roadside cafe in Mugwomp Flats. The roof was made of corrugated steel, but birds had always found it a good place to land after a long trip.

Jake, the mouse in charge of the strip, scowled as his opponent beat him in a game of checkers. It was bad enough to lose, but even worse to be defeated by a fly!

"Wisefly," Jake grumbled in a thick Australian accent. He flipped over the checkerboard, sending the pieces flying. On the opposite side of the checkerboard was a long chart showing pictures of birds. "Albatross landing . . . let's see. . . ." As he began reading aloud, Sparky the fly looked over his shoulder. "Finch, wren, freckled duck, kookaburra, alba— "

Jake dropped the chart. The albatross picture

was huge. "It's a jumbo!" he said, racing across the room with Sparky close behind. Grabbing a microphone, Jake shouted, "Negative, One-Three! You'll have to turn back! Our runway isn't big enough for a bird your size!"

"Look, pal," came Wilbur's defiant voice. "I can land this thing on a dime!"

"Crazy Yank!" Jake said. He and Sparky dashed across the cafe roof. At one end, he kicked off a brick that was attached to a rope. The brick fell, pulling open a folded-up awning. The awning stretched out, extending the roof a few feet.

Wilbur crashed onto the awning just as it opened. He slid across the roof, right toward a billboard at the other end.

Wasting no time, Jake kicked out the billboard's support pin. It swung down, landing on a bus and making a platform.

Wilbur skidded across the billboard, across the bus, and smack onto a picnic table umbrella. He spun around on the umbrella, only to be hurled back onto the roof.

"Quick, Sparky," Jake shouted. "We need to make a dragline!" At the opposite end, he jumped off the roof and onto a full clothesline. Bouncing off the line as if it were a slingshot, he grabbed a hanger. On his way up, he hooked the hanger through a piece of elastic clothing that hung on the line. As he flew through the air, the clothing followed him, stretching across the width of the roof. As the hanger attached to a lightpost, the clothing made a taut line.

And that's what stopped Wilbur from sliding off the roof. When he crashed into the elastic, he was flung backward. Tumbling a few last times, he came to a rest. "Patooie!" he said, scrambling to his feet. "Don't tell me the runway's too short."

Jake pushed a rolling staircase toward Wilbur. "That Yank ought to have his wings clipped," he muttered. Suddenly Jake became speechless. His eyes lit up when he saw Miss Bianca stepping onto the stairs. "Welcome to Australia, ma'am," he said. "My name's Jake, and if there's any way I can make your stay more pleasant, don't hesitate to ask."

Loaded down with his *and* Miss Bianca's luggage, Bernard struggled down the stairs. He glanced at Jake, who was completely ignoring him. "Uh, I've got a lot of luggage here," he said.

Wilbur looked down with a smile. "Here, let me give you a hand." He gingerly picked up the bags. "All part of the friendly service here at Albatross — "

Crrrrack! went Wilbur's back. "Oh!" he cried out in pain. "Big-time hurt . . . oh, boy! Take the bags! Take the bags!"

With Jake's expert guidance, Bernard and Miss Bianca got Wilbur to the local mouse hospital. But there was one problem — it was in an old abandoned ambulance, and Wilbur had to be lowered into it through a hole in the roof.

His body wrapped in ropes, Wilbur looked around in disbelief. "Hey, hey, what are you doing?" he yelled. "Wait a minute! Stop everything!"

Bernard, Miss Bianca, and Jake all watched as a group of mouse nurses controlled the pulleys that let Wilbur down.

"Don't worry, Wilbur," Miss Bianca said. "We'll come back the moment we find the boy."

"Hey, don't leave me here!" Wilbur shouted back. "I'm feeling much better now! I'm ready to hit the beaches! *Mambo-o-o-o* . . ." He tried to do a few dance moves and pulled his back out again. "Yeeoow!"

Bernard, Jake, and Miss Bianca disappeared from sight as Wilbur passed through the roof and landed softly on the hospital floor.

A skinny mouse doctor with thick glasses stood above him in a cherry picker. "Dear boy, you won't feel a thing," he said. Then he called out, "Launch the back brace!"

Wilbur froze. On a nearby platform, three mouse nurses pulled back a wooden cane in a slingshot. With a sharp *zzing*, it shot across the floor and wedged itself under Wilbur's back.

"Ahh! I've been skewered!" he screamed.

The doctor turned back to the nurses and shouted, "Prepare the albatross for medication!"

Suddenly Wilbur forgot his pain. He was being slowly maneuvered into position — with his tail end directly in the line of a shotgun that had been loaded with a hypodermic needle

"Ready?" the doctor called out.

"No!" Wilbur squawked. "I'm not ready! No, please!"

"Aim!"

"Oh, oh, please don't do this to me!"

"Fire!"

7

A few yards away from the hospital, Bernard stopped. He couldn't make heads or tails of his map of the outback. Miss Bianca looked over his shoulder.

Behind them, Jake sat on a rock, fiddling with a boomerang he'd brought along. He smiled at Miss Bianca. "So," he said, "are you and your husband here on a little outback excursion?"

"Oh, we're not married," Miss Bianca said.

Jake smiled broadly.

"We're here on a top-secret mission," Bernard added, still looking at the map. "Very hush-hush."

Jake hopped off the rock. "Oh, are you going to rescue that kid McLeach nabbed?"

"How did you know?" Miss Bianca asked.

"It's hard to keep secrets in the outback, miss," Jake said. "So, which way are you taking? The Suicide Trail through Nightmare Canyon, or the shortcut at Satan's Ridge?"

Bernard gulped. "*Suicide* Trail?"

"Good choice!" Jake snapped. "More snakes but less quicksand. Then, once you cross Bloodworm Creek, you're scot-free — until Dead Dingo Pass."

"Wait a minute!" Bernard said. "I don't see any of those places on the map!"

Jake took the map from Bernard and folded it clumsily. "Well, a map's no good in the outback," he said, giving it back to Bernard. "What you need is someone who knows the territory."

Miss Bianca looked at him admiringly. "Oh, Mister Jake, will you guide us?"

"At your service!" Jake said. "Better take my arm, miss. It's going to be a treacherous hike." He gave her a confident smile. "I remember the time, Miss B., it was just me and four hundred of these giant possums — oh, mean critters they are. . . ."

Four hundred possums? Bernard scowled angrily. As he put his map back into his pocket, he mumbled to himself, "He doesn't even know how to fold a map!"

Somehow he had a feeling that having Jake as a guide wasn't going to be easy.

He was right. Soon the three of them were racing through the outback on the back of a squirrel. Without warning, the squirrel began skittering straight up a tree. Jake held on tightly to Miss Bianca.

But no one held on to Bernard.

"Whoa!" As Bernard fell off, he reached wildly and managed to grab the squirrel's tail.

"This is the only way to travel, eh, Berno?" Jake called over his shoulder.

Suddenly the squirrel leaped off a branch. Spreading its legs, it glided over the trees.

It landed on a sapling, which bent all the way to the ground. Jake and Miss Bianca jumped off.

"Hold it, hold it!" Bernard shouted, frantically trying to get a foothold. "Not yet — "

It was too late. The sapling sprang upward, hurling the squirrel into the air — with Bernard still clutching its tail.

With a muffled *crash*, Bernard landed in a bush. He was covered with burrs and angry as a mad dog.

In the commotion, none of them saw the group of men dredging a nearby river, looking desperately for signs of Cody.

8

Cody never imagined that he'd be shivering in the middle of a hot Australian summer day. But the inside of McLeach's compound was frigid and damp. A fireplace crackled on the opposite wall, but Cody couldn't feel any heat. He tried to get out of his chair, but McLeach had tied him well. His head banged against the map of the outback on the wall behind him. Joanna eyed him lazily from a washtub, popping crackers into her mouth.

A sickening *shink, shink, shink* rang out as McLeach sharpened knives on a whetstone. "Well, boy," he said, grinning, "let's see if we can refresh that rusty old memory of yours."

With a snap of his wrist, McLeach threw a knife in the direction of Cody's head. "Is the eagle on Satan's Ridge?"

Cody ducked away in terror. The knife whizzed by him and embedded itself in the map.

He turned to see where it had landed — exactly

on the spot marked *Satan's Ridge.*

"'Or Nightmare Canyon?" McLeach said.

Another knife zinged past him and stuck in the spot marked *Nightmare Canyon.*

"What do you think, Joanna?" McLeach asked his pet, who snickered gleefully. "Yeah, that's it — right smack dab in the middle, at Croc Falls!"

This throw came right for Cody's head. He ducked.

Voosh! The knife sailed into the map exactly between the words *Croc* and *Falls.*

"Am I getting warm?" McLeach said.

"I told you, I don't remember!" Cody retorted.

McLeach's face was red with anger. "Don't you realize a bird that size is worth a fortune?" He leaned forward and pulled a knife out of the map. "I'll split the money with you, fifty-fifty."

Cody stared back at him. "You won't have any money after the rangers get through with you!"

McLeach clenched his teeth with rage. Slowly he turned toward the fireplace. Hanging over the flames, a big pot of water boiled furiously. He reared his foot back and kicked with all his might.

Boiling water sloshed into the fire, sending a shower of embers into the room.

Joanna sank quietly into her tub. And Cody wondered if he'd ever see his mother again.

9

"Yeouch!" There. Miss Bianca had pulled the last burr from Bernard's sweater. He could relax.

Looking around the riverbank, he saw that the two of them were alone. Jake had disappeared.

Bernard watched Miss Bianca dangle her feet in the river. The afternoon sun lit up every delicate feature of her face. Birds twittered happily.

Now was the perfect time. Bernard pulled the ring box out of his pocket. "You know," he said, "now that we're alone, there's something I've — I've been wanting to, uh, well, to ask you. . . ."

Miss Bianca turned to him. "Yes, what is it?"

Bernard knelt down. "Miss Bianca, I — I would be . . . most honored if you would — "

"Look out!" came Jake's voice behind him.

Swoooooosh! Bernard spun around to see a giant python raising its head out of the water.

Instantly Jake burst out in front of him. Bernard lost his balance and flopped into the water.

"No mice for you, Twister!" Jake said. He threw his lasso around the python's mouth and stared the snake straight in the eye. "I've been looking all over for you! Now look, we've got a long way to go, and you're gonna take us. And you're not going to give us any trouble, right?"

Bernard grabbed onto a tree root to keep from floating away. As Jake helped Miss Bianca onto the python, he looked at Bernard and winked. "They're perfectly harmless once you look them in the eye and let 'em know who's boss — right, mate?"

Bernard scrambled onto the python. In front of him, Jake had his arms wrapped around Miss Bianca.

"Now, git!" Jake ordered. As the python slithered away, he said, "You know, Miss B., I used to be quite a dingo wrestler. Yeah, there was this one time, just me and three hundred of them . . ."

As they glided along the river, Bernard felt soggy and dejected. He took his ring box out of his jacket, dumped water out of the box, and sighed.

CREEEEEAK!

Deep in the abandoned opal mines, McLeach opened a heavy wooden door and shoved Cody inside. Cody stumbled into a cold, dark room, littered with all kinds of junk. Years ago it might have been a mine shaft, but now it was something much different.

A dungeon.

The prisoners were all animals of the outback — a kangaroo and a koala chained to the wall, a platypus in a wooden barrel, a snake in a cage, a kookaburra fenced inside a hanging rubber tire, and many others in shackles and small cages.

On the opposite wall was a large, human-sized cage. McLeach pushed Cody in and slammed the door. "I'll give you a night down here to think it over," McLeach rasped. "But tomorrow, no more Mister Nice Guy!" He spun around and left, with Joanna at his heels. As he slammed the outer door, the room shook. A set of keys jangled on a nail in the wall.

"I'll never tell you where she is!" Cody shouted. "Never!"

"Yeah, we'll never tell!" came a small voice below him. "You'll have to drag it out of us!"

Startled, Cody looked down to see a lizard with a strange, frilled flap of skin around his neck. "Hey, where'd you come from?" he asked.

"The desert," the lizard replied.

"Well, well," came the koala's voice from across the room. "Looks like McLeach has begun trapping his own kind. There's no hope for any of us now."

"No hope?" the lizard said, pacing frantically.

"There must be a way out of here!" Cody said.

"Oh, there is," the koala said. He pointed to the kangaroo. "You'll go as a wallet, Red." Then he pointed at the platypus. "And you, Polly, you'll go as a belt. And our dear Frank," he said, looking at the frill-necked lizard, "will go as a purse!"

"*Noooo*, Krebbs!" Frank shrieked. "I don't want to go as a purse! Please, don't let them do it!"

Cody held Frank gently. "Don't worry, we're going to get out of here. If we all put our heads together, I'm sure we'll think of something."

"Yeah, something . . . something . . ." Frank scrunched up his face and began to grunt and sweat.

"Oh, here we go," Krebbs said. "He's thinking."

"Easy, mate," Red added. "You don't want to hurt yourself again."

"Ngggggh!" Frank groaned. Finally his eyes popped open wide. "I got it! All we have to do is get the keys!"

Krebbs rolled his eyes. "Oh, is that all? Well, then, we'd better start packing our bags."

"No, wait — he's right!" Cody said. He looked at the junk around the room, which included the slats of an old wooden fence. "If we could get some long pieces of wood . . . come on, everybody!"

One by one, the animals pitched in to help. The kookaburra swung her tire into the fence, knocking it right into Cody's outstretched hand. Then

Red used her tail to knock a hooked pole toward Cody.

"That's it!" Cody said, holding two fence slats and the pole. "Now I need to tie it together!"

The snake curled its tail around a nearby boot and flung it to him. "Shoelaces!" Cody said happily. He tied the slats and the pole together to make one long hook. It looked *almost* long enough to reach the keys on the wall clear across the room.

He stuck it through his cage and pushed it across the room. The hook slowly made its way toward the doorknob. It rested on an electrical cord that Krebbs had stretched across the room.

"Yeah, yeah, yeah," Frank said breathlessly. All the animals' eyes were riveted on the hook.

It was getting heavy now, and Cody was holding the top. He gave it one last thrust.

It brushed against the keys and fell.

"It's okay," Cody said. "Let's try again."

"Yeah, yeah, yeah, yeah, yeah," Frank panted.

"Will someone shut him up?" Krebbs complained.

Frank ignored him. "No, no, yeah, yeah . . ."

With a solid *chink*, the hook lifted the key ring off. The weight of the keys made Cody's contraption droop, banging against a small "doggy door" at the bottom of the wall. "We did it!" Cody shouted.

The other animals cheered wildly. "Yeah!" Frank screamed. "You got it, you got it, you got it!"

Or so he thought. As Cody tried to draw the keys toward him, the "doggy door" flew open.

The room fell silent as Joanna barged in. Angrily she snatched the keys and put them back on the wall. Then she smashed Cody's pole to bits.

With a smug grin, Joanna spun around and calmly went back through her door. As she pulled it shut, it echoed hollowly. No one said a word.

Except Frank.

"I got it!" he blurted out. "I'll just take my tail and pick the lock . . . like this!" He inserted his tail into the keyhole, twisting and turning it.

"Aw, Frank, give it a rest," Red said.

Cody exhaled and sat heavily on the floor. This wasn't going to be so easy.

10

As Cody sat in his prison, Jake and the Rescuers sped through the woods — on the backs of three fireflies.

Jake led them through a dandelion field. "Show 'em who's boss, Berno!" he hollered.

Bernard's firefly brushed against the dandelions. Seeds flew into the air.

"*Ah-choo!*" Bernard sneezed, causing the firefly to shoot downward into the nearby river.

They came out, soaked. For the rest of the trip, the firefly sputtered on and off.

"There has to be an easier way," Bernard said to himself.

Back in the mouse hospital at Mugwomp Flats, Wilbur's eyes flickered open. "Oh, I feel like my head is in a vise!" he mumbled, waking up.

When his eyes cleared, he tried to move his head. It *was* in a vise. The mouse doctor was still there, too, looking at an X-ray print. "All right," he called out to the nurses, "give me the heavy-duty epidermal tissue disrupter!"

"Heavy-duty *whaaat?*" Wilbur said.

He soon found out. Hoisted by ropes, the "disrupter" rose above him. His mouth dropped open when he saw what it was.

A chainsaw.

As the doctor reached for the cord, Wilbur screamed, "Nooooo!" With incredible strength he stood up, taking the vise with him. He sprinted across the room, ignoring the vise, the ropes around his body, and the cane jammed against his back.

Weeeooooo! An alarm went off. PATIENT ESCAPING signs flashed left and right. "Mister Albatross!" the doctor shouted. "We haven't operated yet!"

"You gotta catch me first!" Wilbur retorted. Out of the corner of his eye he spotted an open window. *Freedom!* He took a flying leap —

Thhhgunnk! Halfway through, he got stuck.

Twisting and straining, he tried to squeeze himself out. "You'll never take me alive!"

Behind him, the doctor and a nurse each grabbed a leg. "Please don't do this!" the doctor said. "Your spine needs tender loving care!"

With that, he and the nurse gave a final heave. Wilbur fell back into the hospital and landed on top of the doctor. Quickly he rose to his feet. His face was pinched with pain. "Oh! Oh, my back!"

But it felt different now. In fact, there *was* no pain! Something had happened when he was pulled out of that window.

Wilbur began to dance with joy. "Hey, it works! I'm cured! I owe you plenty on this one, Doc!"

"Quite," the doctor said dryly.

Whooping at the top of his lungs, Wilbur ran out the hospital door and flew into the air. On a scale of one to ten, Wilbur felt like a ten-and-a-half. "Here I come, you two little mice!" he shouted. "Albatross Air is back on the job!"

Below him, a ranger knocked on the door of a small house in the outback. Cody's mom opened the door, her face lined with worry. Bowing his head slightly, the ranger gave her Cody's backpack. It looked pretty chewed up.

Her knees buckled as she grabbed the pack to her chest. She began to cry. She felt completely alone.

11

Joanna snored peacefully in McLeach's living room. Slumped in his armchair, McLeach was deep in thought. "I gotta get that boy to talk," he finally said. Then he hopped to his feet. "I'm hungry. Can't think on an empty stomach. Gotta have protein. Gotta have eggs."

Joanna perked up at the mention of her favorite food. She slithered after McLeach.

McLeach took a toolbox and put it on a counter. "Everyone's got his price. . . ." Turning away, he began pacing the floor. "All I have to do is offer him whatever he wants and then not give it to him. . . ."

Joanna quickly jumped up and opened the box with her snout. There were at least a dozen eggs inside. Greedily her tongue lashed out and grabbed one.

The moment she popped it into her mouth, McLeach spun around. "Did you take one of my eggs? These are not Joanna eggs!" he thundered.

He slammed the box shut and went to his stove. "Let's see, if I could just find the boy's weak spot, I could get him to tell me where the eagle is . . . but he's only *got* one weak spot, and that's the eagle!" He turned around and spotted Joanna slinking away from his box, which was now empty.

He picked up the box and reared back to throw it. "Joanna!" he roared, "I give you platypus eggs, I give you snake eggs. I even give you eagle eggs . . . but I want you to stay away from my — "

Suddenly he cut himself off. An idea popped into his head like a thunderclap. "That's it!" he said. "That's the boy's weak spot!"

Down in the dungeon, Cody and the animals were half asleep — except Frank. He was still trying to open the cage door with his tail. "And you push it a little and take it back a little and turn . . ."

Creeeak. He had been at it so long, he didn't notice when the door slowly opened. He didn't even notice himself swinging along with it. But he did notice his poor, mangled tail. "I give up!" he said, kicking the door shut. "I'll never get this!"

The slam woke everyone up.

"Hey, look," Red said. "Frank's out!"

"Frank!" Cody shouted. "You're free!"

The truth dawned on Frank slowly. "I'm free?" He began to dance around the dungeon. "I'm free!

I'm free! Free, free, free! Look at me!"

"Frank, quiet!" Cody urged. "Go get the keys!"

"The keys," Frank said, looking over his shoulder. "Yeah, yeah . . ." He ran to the opposite wall and reached upward, but the keys were too high.

All together, the others shouted, "Quick, get something to stand on!"

"Yeah! Stand on something. . . ." Frank skittered back across the room.

"This ought to be rich," Krebbs said.

Frank snatched a thin plank of wood that was near a wooden box. He ran back, plopped the plank under the keys, and tried to reach again.

"Frank!" Cody called out. "Use the box!"

"The box!" Frank said. "Of course, the box . . . climb on the box. . . ." Grunting with the effort, he pushed the box into place and climbed on top. He stood on tiptoes and reached . . . and reached . . .

There. His fingertips brushed the keys off the nail. They fell to the box with a loud jangle.

"Ssssshh!" Cody and the animals said.

Dead silence hung in the room as they looked at Joanna's door. No one dared to breathe.

But the door didn't open. Carefully Frank climbed down and grabbed the keys. He tiptoed past the door, slowly lifting each foot. . . .

Clanggg! When he was directly in front, Joanna's head popped out.

"Yiiiiii!" Frank screamed. He sped away with Joanna at his heels.

"The keys!" Red yelled. "Give us the keys!"

Screeching, Frank dove into a pile of boxes in the corner. Joanna dove in after him.

SSPPLLLLLLACK! The corner filled with dust and splinters as the boxes crashed to the floor.

Joanna emerged, howling — with the key ring around her snout and Frank on her back!

Frank held onto the ring and rode Joanna like a bucking bronco.

"Ride 'em, Frank!" Red shouted.

A smile spread across Frank's face. "Ee-hah!" he called out. "Howdy-howdy-howdy!"

Joanna swung her leathery tail and caught Frank in the back. He flew off, still clutching the keys.

He hit the ground running. "Let me in! Let me in!" he called out, gripping the bars of his own cage. Then he dropped the keys and began trying his tail in the cage's keyhole.

Cody didn't have time to remind him he had the keys. "Frank, look out!" he yelled. "Behind you!"

Joanna was inches away. Frank took off like a gunshot. Cody reached out between the bars of the cage and picked up the keys. Quietly he inserted them into the lock and turned.

The door opened easily and he scampered out.

Across the room, Frank hopped onto a table. The only thing on it was a shotgun. It pointed upward, its butt on the table and its barrel leaning against the wall. Frank scrambled up the barrel and perched at the top.

Joanna swatted upward, trying to reach him. Her foot caught in the shotgun's trigger.

And that's when Frank realized where he was. He let out a piercing shriek and jumped off.

The shotgun began to fall. Joanna tried to let go, but her claw was stuck. With a deafening *kaboom*, the gun fired.

Joanna hurtled backward across the room. She landed in an empty cage, which slammed shut.

Frank gulped. Inches from his head were a number of black holes in the wall. "Missed . . ." he said weakly.

Cody ran to Polly's cage and began trying the keys. A large shadow passed over him, but he was too busy to notice.

"Surprise!" Suddenly Cody felt a hand jerk his arm back.

McLeach!

"Well," McLeach continued, pushing his face into Cody's, "if I didn't know better, I'd think you didn't like it here!"

Cody struggled with all his strength, but McLeach dragged him across the room. McLeach's eyes darted over to the corner, where

Frank was cowering. "What are you doing out of your cage?"

Frank darted into his cage and slammed the door shut. At the other side of the room, Joanna slid out of her cage and walked behind her master.

"That's better," McLeach said.

"Let me go, let me go, let me go!" Cody protested, trying to pull away.

McLeach held fast. "Come on, boy. Say goodbye to your friends. It's the last time you'll ever see them!"

12

Bernard, Jake, and Miss Bianca stood in front of McLeach's underground compound. Its massive steel door was shut tight.

But Bernard had gone too far to give up. He picked up three twigs and handed one each to Jake and Miss Bianca. "Here," he said. "Start digging."

They all tried, but trying to dig under that door with sticks was like trying to build a castle out of pudding. It was hopeless.

Finally, with a smirk, Jake said, "Uh, has anyone considered trying 'open sesame'?"

RRRRAWWKK! Suddenly the bottom of the door began to swing upward.

The three mice couldn't believe their eyes. Quickly they hopped onto the door and hung on.

As the bottom rose higher and higher, they peered over. Three figures stood below them in the opening — McLeach, Cody, and Joanna.

"Get out of here!" McLeach told Cody. "Go!"

Cody looked at him as if he were crazy. "Huh?"

McLeach tossed Cody's pocketknife back to him. "It's all over, boy. Your bird's dead. Someone shot her — shot her right out of the sky! *Bang!*"

Cody backed away, horrified. "No!" he said.

"You calling me a liar?" McLeach growled. "I heard it on the radio this morning. And she could have been mine if it weren't for you!" He pointed angrily toward the outback. "Now you had better get out of here before I change my mind. Go on — git!"

On top of the door, Bernard turned to Jake. "Why is he letting him go?"

"It's got to be a trick," Jake answered.

They watched Cody run away from the compound. "Too bad about those eggs, eh, Joanna?" McLeach said loudly. "They'll never survive without their mother! Oh, well . . ."

Cody stopped for a second when he heard the words. Then he took off, faster than before.

Miss Bianca turned to her two friends. "Bird?"

"Eggs?" Bernard said.

"Ssh!" Jake interrupted. "Listen!"

The door shook as the Bushwacker loudly rumbled through. In the front seat, McLeach had his binoculars trained on Cody.

"I don't know what he's doing," Jake said, "but we can't let him get away!"

They jumped onto the Bushwacker. Jake landed at the top of the crane, but Bernard and Miss Bianca jumped too late. They slid down the slanted crane arm — right into the Bushwacker's moving treads!

"Oh, no!" Bernard shouted. If they stayed on the treads, they'd be crushed. If they jumped off, they'd fail their mission. Unless . . .

The grooves in the treads! They could hide there, Bernard realized. He pushed Miss Bianca into one and jumped in after her.

They stayed there, safe and sound, as the Bushwacker trundled onward. When they rolled around to the top again, they heard Jake's voice. "Bernard! Miss Bianca! Catch!"

Jake's lasso dropped next to them and they grabbed it. Jake hoisted them up to his new hiding place, a platform under the Bushwacker's chassis.

They stayed there as the Bushwacker tracked Cody across the outback. McLeach made sure to keep his distance so Cody wouldn't hear a thing.

The vehicle rolled into a clearing next to the canyon. Jake saw a shock of blond hair disappearing over the canyon's edge. "He went over the cliff!" he whispered. "Come on, we have to warn him."

They jumped off the Bushwacker and ran to the edge. Looking over, they saw Cody in Marahute's nest, sadly covering her eggs with a feather.

Swiftly they scrambled down. "Cody!" Miss Bianca called out.

"Huh?" Cody looked up. "Who are you?"

As they plopped into the nest, Miss Bianca said, "There's no time to explain. You're in danger!"

But Cody wasn't listening. His eye had caught something on the horizon — an eagle flying gracefully toward them.

He couldn't believe his eyes. "Marahute . . . it can't be!" He jumped out of the nest and ran to the edge of the cliff ledge.

The three mice chased after him. "Cody! Cody, wait!" Miss Bianca shouted.

Cody was glowing with happiness. "She's alive!"

"McLeach is on the cliff!" Bernard yelled.

Finally Cody heard. He looked up and saw the Bushwacker jutting over the cliff. On it was a crane with a rocket launcher — pointed straight at Marahute!

Cody spun around and cupped his hands to his mouth. "Marahute, no!" he shouted. "Turn back!"

BOOOM! It was too late. The rocket fired, sending out a balled-up net at the end of a long rope. The net shot toward Marahute, unfurling. It was weighted on each corner by a heavy rock.

Marchute screeched as the net covered her. The rocks swung around her body, folding her into the net. They came together and twisted up into a knot. She was locked in.

McLeach's voice echoed through the canyon. "Did you see that? Perfect shot! She's mine!"

The net swung toward the cliff, dangling below

the Bushwacker. It was a few feet from the nest. Cody looked down. The canyon bottom was a *long* way, but he didn't care. He took a flying leap.

His fingertips just barely grasped the net. He hung there, dangling over the canyon.

Jake took out his lasso and threw it. The loop sailed into the air and caught Cody's foot.

"Hold tight, you two," Jake said. "We're going for a ride!"

He tossed the rope to the others. Miss Bianca grabbed it first. Bernard reached out, but it slipped between his fingers.

Miss Bianca and Jake were whisked off the ledge, leaving Bernard behind. "Miss Bianca!" Bernard called out, but his voice was lost in the wind.

As McLeach pulled the net upward, Cody was determined to free Marahute. He took out his pocketknife and began cutting the net open.

McLeach must have seen him. Immediately the net started shaking violently. Cody lost his grip. Desperately he kicked his foot toward the net — the foot that was tied to Jake's rope.

His toe caught in the net. "Help!" he cried, dangling upside down. "I'm slipping!"

Jake and Miss Bianca scrambled onto the net. "Cody, don't move!" Miss Bianca said. Quickly Jake wrapped his rope around Cody's foot extra-tight to make sure he didn't fall.

13

*C*rrrrunch!

Joanna pulled the egg away. It hadn't even cracked. She tried another egg.

"Joanna!" McLeach blared from above. "You hurry up and eat those eggs and get your tail up here!"

Joanna wasn't going to risk losing her teeth. Glumly she flicked her tail at the eggs. They fell off the side and into the canyon.

As McLeach lifted Joanna back up, she sulked the whole way. In the distance, a bird flew toward the cliff but Joanna didn't even look at it.

If she had, she would have seen Wilbur zooming toward the ledge with a grin on his face. "Hey! Where is everybody?" he shouted, landing on the empty nest. "I could have sworn I heard something going on up here!"

In a hole beneath the nest, Bernard looked up. Beside him were all of Marahute's *real* eggs. He was thrilled that the rocks he'd put in the nest had fooled Joanna. Now he couldn't believe what he was hearing. "Wilbur?" he said, sticking his head out.

"Yeeeaggh!" Wilbur screeched, falling over the ledge. Moments later his head peered back over at Bernard. "Don't ever do that to me again."

"Wilbur, am I glad to see you! Will you give me a hand with these eggs?"

As Wilbur helped take the eggs out, Bernard explained everything that had happened. Wilbur listened, then shook his head and said, "We have to do something. Bernard, I'm disappointed in you, hiding under a nest when Miss Bianca needs our help. Now, you should start searching the desert for her and I'll . . . I'll ask the chicks at the beach — "

"Wilbur!" Bernard interrupted. "There are some chicks right here that need your help."

"Really?" Wilbur said, his eyes aglow.

Bernard pointed to the eggs, which were all back in the nest. "They need somebody to sit on them."

"Oh, no!" Wilbur said, shocked. "Don't look at me like that. Don't even think — "

Bernard sat on an egg and patted another.

Wilbur turned his back. "No, you understand? No! I will not *ever* sit on those eggs!"

But as Bernard climbed toward the top of the cliff, he left Marahute's precious eggs warmly covered by Albatross Air, "the finest fleet on two webbed feet."

The Bushwacker rumbled through the outback. McLeach chuckled happily and looked over his shoulder at Cody. "I almost forgot," he said to Joanna, "we got a loose end to tie up!"

Cody slumped to the floor. Beside him, Jake, Miss Bianca, and Marahute were silent.

"Don't worry," Miss Bianca said softly. "Bernard is still out there. He'll never give up!"

14

M iss Bianca was right. Miles behind them, Bernard was running along the Bushwacker's tracks. He followed them up a steep hill, huffing and puffing. When he looked over the top, he could see the tracks disappearing into the distance.

There wasn't even a trace of engine noise. Bernard knew he had a long way to go.

He dropped to the ground, exhausted. His chest heaved up and down as he caught his breath.

Hhhhhhocckkkk . . . phhewww . . .
Hhhhhhocckkkk . . . phhewww . . .

He must have been running faster than he'd thought. His breathing sounded like a buzzsaw.

Hhhhhhocckkkk . . . phhewww . . .

Bernard looked around. That noise *couldn't* be coming from him.

Hhhhhhocckkkk . . . phhewww . . .

It wasn't. Asleep near him was one of the ugliest

animals he'd ever seen. It looked like a thin warthog with tusks.

Bernard recognized it — a razorback hog. And it just might be the answer to his problem.

He walked over to it timidly. Those tusks looked sharp . . . what if it woke up and attacked? Then he'd *really* be no help to Miss Bianca.

The thought of Miss Bianca gave Bernard new strength. If he didn't do *something*, he'd never forgive himself.

He remembered the way Jake had handled the python. Then, taking a deep breath, he reached out and grabbed the razorback's tusks. He stared the razorback in the eye. "Now look, I've got a long way to go," he said. "You're going to take me there and you're not going to give me any trouble, right?"

To his amazement, the razorback whined and nodded.

"Good," Bernard said, climbing on top of him. "Now git!"

This was it — Cody knew it. He'd never see his mom again, never walk in the outback, never play with his animal friends. As McLeach lowered him over Croc Falls with the crane, Cody said silent good-byes to them all.

McLeach cackled. "Ha, ha, ha! It's time you learned to fish for crocs! They like it when you use live bait — and you're as live as they come!"

The Bushwacker's engine moaned. McLeach turned a spotlight on Cody to light him up in the afternoon shadow. Crocodiles began slithering into the water.

"That's right, babies!" McLeach yelled. "It's suppertime!"

In the cage, Marahute couldn't bear the sight. She let out a desperate screech.

"It don't look good, Miss B.," Jake said, shaking his head.

Miss Bianca looked out the back of the cage. "Oh, Bernard," she said. "Please hurry."

Splash!

Cody's eyes were closed when he hit the water. He couldn't see the crocodiles but he knew they were coming. Even underwater, he could hear McLeach's hysterical laughter.

Suddenly he was jerked upward. He hung in the air, coughing. The crocodiles below him snapped their jaws furiously — they didn't like having their dinner snatched away.

"Hey, nothing personal, boy," McLeach shouted to Cody, "but I wouldn't want to disappoint the rangers. They were looking so hard for you — and now they're going to find you!"

With that, Cody dropped downward for the last time. Now the crocs were waiting with open mouths. This time he knew he wouldn't even hit the water.

He'd be swallowed before he could get there.

15

Silence.

McLeach looked at his control panel. No lights. He pulled the electronic crane lever. He adjusted the spotlight.

Nothing. The Bushwacker's engine had stopped dead.

He looked over the cliff. Cody's rope was still. He hung just inches above the crocodiles. They jumped and snapped their jaws in vain.

"What the blazes is going on here?" McLeach said.

Out of the corner of his eye, he saw a strange animal run out from under the Bushwacker. What on earth was a *razorback* doing there?

"Joanna!" McLeach roared. "Did you know there was a razorback in my truck? Quit playing around and do your job!"

As Joanna ran off to sniff around the vehicle, McLeach reached for the ignition keys. They were gone. "Something weird's going on around here," he muttered.

Below him, Bernard hid in the shadow of the gas pedal, clutching the keys. When McLeach turned away, he jumped through a hole in the floor.

He landed on the ground and ran to the side of the Bushwacker.

Miss Bianca's eyes lit up when she saw him. "Look! It's Bernard!"

"I don't believe it," Jake said. "Way to go, mate!"

"Here! Catch!" Bernard shouted, throwing the keys up to them.

Miss Bianca reached out and caught them. And Bernard caught *her* adoring smile.

The sound of frantic footsteps made him turn around. Joanna was charging at him. He ran off in a panic, scurrying into a hollow log.

In the cage, Jake and Miss Bianca began climbing toward the lock. But the keys were heavy and the gate was at the very top. . . .

BLAMMM!

At the sound of the gunshot, Jake and Miss Bianca stopped.

Marahute screeched.

Bernard peeked out of his log.

Cody, still suspended over the water, looked up.

High atop the crane, McLeach lowered his shotgun. "Blast it!" he said, taking aim once again at the rope holding Cody. He cocked the gun and fired.

This time, his bullet grazed Cody's rope. Now Cody was hanging by a few thin strands.

McLeach howled with laughter. "Adding a little sport to it, eh?" He danced a jig, then fired some more.

Bullets whizzed by the rope and splashed in the water. The rope was about to break. Cody did the only thing he could think of — scream!

Bernard heard him. Thinking fast, he ran out of his log and sneaked up behind Joanna. Then he reared back his fist and socked her.

Joanna whipped around. Her eyes blazed with anger. She took off after Bernard, ready to kill.

Bernard headed straight for McLeach. They plowed smack into him. He screamed in surprise — but not before getting off another shot.

Joanna, McLeach, and Bernard splashed into the river.

The crocodiles swam eagerly toward them. Shaking with fright, Joanna jumped on her master. "You stupid lizard!" McLeach sputtered. "Get off me!"

Bernard swam toward the riverbank. He fought the current and managed to yank himself out.

At that moment, the frayed rope holding Cody broke. He didn't even have time to shout as he plunged into the raging river.

16

Bernard was in a panic. He looked up. Jake and Miss Bianca were still struggling to unlock the cage door. He looked at Cody, who was thrashing in the water. The crocodiles had gone after McLeach, but any second they would see Cody. . . .

He didn't have time to think it out. He ran down a branch that stuck out over the river, then dove back in. Swimming with all his might, he headed for Cody.

"Help!" Cody screamed.

The current was too fast for Bernard to catch up. He could only reach the rope that trailed behind Cody. Grabbing it, he swam toward the shore.

Cody felt himself being pulled against the current. He looked behind him. With amazement, he saw Bernard pull him toward the riverbank and tie the rope to a root.

Farther down the river, McLeach fought off the

crocodiles with his bare hands. "No . . . no!" he cried. "Get back . . . get, get away!"

To his surprise, the crocs seemed to obey. All together, they dove under the water and swam back upstream. A smile came across McLeach's face. "Go on, run, you yellow-bellied crocs!" he called out. "I whupped ya! You'll think twice before — "

On the opposite bank, Joanna was waving at him slowly. McLeach didn't like the look on her face — like someone saying good-bye to a loved one forever.

He spun around in the water. His eyes bulged open. Now he knew why the crocs had swum away. Now he understood the look on Joanna's face.

He was heading for Croc Falls!

As he was flung over the falls, his scream was lost in the rushing water.

Cody breathed a sigh of relief. Now all he had to do was swim from the root and —

CRRRRACK! Too late. The root ripped out of the riverbank. In an instant, Cody was racing toward the waterfall, with Bernard close behind!

17

*C*lick.
    The lock was open. Jake and Miss Bianca pushed open the lid of the cage. Beside them, Marahute began to ruffle her feathers.

The two mice jumped onto the eagle's broad shoulders. "Fly free, Marahute!" Miss Bianca said.

In the river, time had run out for Cody and Bernard. They shot over the waterfall. For a moment they seemed to hover over the churning spray. Cody closed his eyes. They started tumbling downward . . . downward. . . .

Then there was impact.

But it wasn't with the water. Cody opened his eyes. Something surrounded his chest, something besides the rope.

Eagle claws! Cody looked upward at his old pal, Marahute. He had never been so happy in his life.

As Marahute shredded his ropes with her other

claw, Cody heard a small shout. He looked down to see Bernard hanging onto his ankle.

Cody reached down and scooped up his mouse friend. Bernard waved happily.

Marahute soared upward, over the clouds. She helped Bernard, then Cody onto her back. There, Jake and Miss Bianca were waiting.

Miss Bianca flew into Bernard's arms. "Oh, Bernard, you were magnificent! You are absolutely the hero of the day!"

Bernard smiled.

Suddenly he pushed her away. This adventure had changed him, taught him something about bravery. He now had the strength to do something he couldn't do before. Holding her at arm's length, he said, "Miss Bianca, before anything *else* happens — will you marry me?"

Miss Bianca looked at him. For a moment Bernard thought she might laugh in his face. She might say she was engaged to Jake. She might —

"Bernard," Miss Bianca said, looking him deeply in the eyes, "of course I will."

As they hugged again, Jake and Cody watched, beaming.

With a mighty thrust of her wings, Marahute burst through the clouds and into the light of the rising moon.

You'll love

Walt Disney's

CLASSICS

Based on the Walt Disney Movies!

Remember how much you loved Walt Disney movies? Now's your chance to read all the Disney Classics! You'll love these fantastic stories…starring your favorite Disney characters and illustrated with photos taken directly from the movie!

Read them all!

☐	NC41450-X	**Lady and the Tramp**	$2.50
☐	NC42988-4	**The Little Mermaid**	$2.50
☐	NC41913-7	**Peter Pan**	$2.50
☐	NC41664-2	**Bambi**	$2.50
☐	NC42049-6	**Oliver & Company**	$2.50
☐	NC43516-7	**The Jungle Book**	$2.50

1989 The Walt Disney Company

Available wherever you buy books…or use the coupon below.

Scholastic Inc. P.O. Box 7502, 2932 E. McCarty Street, Jefferson City, MO 65102

Please send me the books I have checked above. I am enclosing $_____

(please add $2.00 to cover shipping and handling). Send check or money order-no cash or C. O. D. s please.

Name_____

Address_____

City_____ State/Zip_____

Please allow four to six weeks for delivery. Offer good in U.S.A. only. Sorry, mail orders are not available to residents of Canda. Prices subject to change.   WD1089